Pillow Banking

Aisebiogun Okoebor

Preface

This is a short story with a setting in the late 1990s – early 2000s in Nigeria. It is a tale of corruption, decaying infrastructures of government, erosion of values, the various mix of tradition, the peoples and their ways of life in their day to day close existence as one people using the medium of fiction.

It makes use of easy language to tell a complicated tale in a relaxing funny form. It is a serious tale that borrows from the history of the Nigerian nation, her faltering steps at nation-building, it's a dynamic mix of cultures mixed in the cauldron of western independence and the yet to be perfect brew from the cauldron of nationhood.

It is a tale easy to relate with, especially with all those born before, during and after the time depicted as it makes use of history, facts, and figures in relaying this tale of the colossus called Nigeria with its clay feet and its pervasive cloak of corruption and diverse values.

It tells of a struggling rail system, a dead national air carrier, a journey, and a tale that occurs while traveling via rail and its fallout.

This story was written many years back and only got dusted and sent in for printing because of the punch, it carries.

My profound thanks to all those that made this tale possible and to reach its many diverse audience.

Dr. Sunday Aisebiogun Okoebor

This miter-shaped edifice with a sorry looking clock jutting out horizontally like a lollypop from the main entrance into the building is the Iddo Railway Terminus. It has seen better days as the stiff striking hands of the old clock attests.

Everything about this building is old, so it could be said to be an old house with old furniture, old trains running on old cold rails. Even the workers behaved like old men; they took their time. A true house of antiques! To this old house I went on a cold Monday morning with my bags for my first baptism of rail-fever. The decision to travel by train from Lagos to Zaria was born out of curiosity and a need to satisfy myself as one that have travelled by road, by air, by sea and now to crown it all, by rail.

I had shuttled between Lagos and Benin City practically at will and most times by air, not because I was rich but because my uncle happened to have been a staff of the Airways. One of the many benefits a staff of the Airways gets to enjoy is a ridiculously low rebate on air tickets for self and family; even members of the extended family. I heard a story once of how an Alhaji with the

Airways had caused to be registered, his four wives, two concubines, sixteen children and some members of the extended family as members of his immediate family.

Usually, any staff desirous of taking advantage of the air ticket rebate system furnishes the Airways with the names, photographs, ages and other particulars of the members of his family; at which they are individually issued with staff family identity cards – which entitles them to fly care the Airways on any of its routes with staff tickets.

Somehow within me, I knew that it just couldn't last. It was too good to be true. Every staff saw the national carrier as a big domesticated elephant to be used to serve self first and then the government; after all, the staff – being the people were the government and they were only taking a slice from the national cake.

The founding fathers of the Airways could be said to have been visionaries – if for nothing else, for adopting the elephant as a mascot and symbol of its enormous stupidity in creating a flying elephant that was green in every sense of the word.

Sure, the elephant flew for a while on borrowed wings before finally falling prey to the gravitational pull of tribalism, nepotism, favoritism and greed. The elephant fell, crashed and left such a crater that it broke the backbone and patience of its financiers. Staffs were laid off – including Uncle Dave. The remaining families of Green Elephants' were hunted down with a determination by its creditors to practical extinction.

Anywhere the elephant managed to fly to; it was seized and shackled by the strengthened chains of litigations – provided by aggrieved creditors.

So gradually, the good times came to an abrupt end as the elephant slumped on its broken borrowed wings and was cannibalized, stripped to the bones by an army of soldier ants. All subsequent attempts made to resuscitate the Flying Elephant failed, even with the mascot and symbol of the Airways changed from that of a ponderously ill-fitted creature for flight to that of an eagle for a mascot. So, the eagle perched and shrieked in anguish as it could not lift the elephant off its haunches; and thus the Airways died. Filched passenger packaged lunches vanished from Uncle Dave's household and alternatives means of transportation were patronized by Nigerians; especially those who had at one time or the other been proud flying aboard the elephant decked in national colors – thus my decision to travel by train. A journey that would have been made under an hour had the elephant found the wings of an eagle strong enough to carry its woes. I have opted to crawl in discomfort for two days through the faeces clogged route a pride of elephants have once trampled in glee. Yes, I chose the rail out of curiosity and sympathy for my pockets.

This would be my first travel by train and 1 was looking forward to the experience; with mixed feelings. In fact, I was so anxious not to miss the only Kano bound train leaving lddo – terminus that Monday morning that I got to the station as early as 7:15am. I managed to pull, drag and shove my rather bulky bags to the ticketing counter only to be told that the sale of tickets to Kano bound passengers would commence at 10:00am and not before, and so I had to kill time, and the Railway Authorities wishing to help passengers like my person while away time had installed a video – machine which was then showing a Chinese film. Well, I took a seat after dumping my bags close-by and joined the filling crowd of passengers at the station then. It looked as if only novices like my person with no idea of the trains' time – table had made the station that early for the station itself was just waking up to a busy day. A sweeper swept away with unhurried strokes the wrapper, tissues and I couldn't but notice the so many leaves - the broad type used in the wrapping of local delicacies like 'Eko', 'Agidi', 'Eba' any 'Eba' that escapes this mode of wrapping usually got a coat of cellophane for wrapper and this was also in abundant evidence.

10:00am finally came after the Chinese have fought and kicked themselves to a gory resolution, and with that, the windows opened, tickets were stacked and sold to the queue that would go in so many directions in a hurried crawl. I got a window-seat in the third class compartment and got ready for the two-day crawl to Zaria, enroute

Kano. The boarding, scrambling for seats and settling down was not that remarkable, but what was, was the stuffiness.

The stuffiness in the coach got worse and worse with each stop at stations. This steel snake sure was voracious! It gobbled women and wares, men and mendicants, it took in so much that the aisle ceased to exist. To move about, one first clambers on to the armrests that demarcated the aisles, then you become a siren, a human siren that warns nodding heads and sleeping elbows to create footholds for the body in transit. By the time we got to Ibadan, even the toilets were no more; they have been turned, not by the wave of a wand, but by the selfish intent of people into storage holds for goods.

I remember the man by my side complaining to the lady he boarded the train with that he had a running stomach. I recall his having managed to chart a tortuous course to the erstwhile toilet only to discover that the WC was buried under cartons and cartons of only God and the owner knows what. The man in annoyance shouted that if in one minute the cartons were not removed then he would not hesitate mounting the cartons and doing his 'thing' right on top of them at which an ljebu woman jumped up from her seat and dared the man. She even went so far as to boast that she promised the man a time-span of nothing more than three days before his dirty anus was dislodged permanently like that of a dog with piles.

Of course, the passengers took sides. Some told the man to go right ahead with his 'coup-de-grace', myself included since the woman that was responsible was so unfeeling that she, not content with inconveniencing other seated passengers by constructing a throne-like pile of her goods right on the aisle on which she was squatting like a brooding hen, had even a higher, bigger and more troublesome throne in the toilet. Some abused the woman and even told her to shut-up. An lbo man having a corner seat at the extreme had even shouted without of course having seen the offending cartons,

"No mind am, my friend, come on; climb on top and do your thing. How she go load the whole train with 'garri' and fish?"

We all laughed at his x-ray vision that saw 'garri' in cartons and not in bags, but more because to us, it was really funny. The woman herself did not help matters by having been caught with her hand in a bowl of 'garri' and fish she was demolishing then by the man's outburst of, "Who get these cartons. Wo! I only give the owner one minute, only one minute before I shit put."

Her tongue did not spare the 'yonmirin' (a derisive name Yoruba usually calls an Ibo) who dared ridicule her 'garri' and fish either. The man took the advice of trying the other coaches before farting his way into the court's disfavor but promised the woman that if he tries the next two and discovers them to be in the same state, he wouldn't hesitate coming back and making good his word. So he went while the Ibo man and the Ijebu woman continued their banter, which was rather lively.

'Garri don spoil una finish. I sure say na garri una dey even shit commot for body'.

"Lef am, you dis 'yonmirin' 'a je o kuta ma momi' you lucky say no bi you wan shit. I for show you say I come from Ijebu land."

"Wetin you go do, infact, me I wan shit now!"

As if to assert this discovery, he shamelessly releases a terrific trumpeter of a fart and makes ready to clamber on to the armrest. Amidst curses and jolly cries muffled by palms and handkerchiefs clamped over noses and mouths, another man chipped in,

"You no go beg am? He never shit, him mess dey smell like mortuary, if he come shit nko? Especially on your 'garri' and fish? You no know say na racial riot you go cause for market for upper North there when them see say you wan come sell them Ijebu 'garri' wey Ibo man don baptise with 'okrika' shit and 'isi-ewu' water?"

Before the woman could boil-out with her salvo however, the action man made his way back, forced the toilet door open and immediately locked it after him, at which the Ijebu woman must have flown down the jammed aisle and was at the door in a minute banging away. In no time, she transformed herself into a generalissimo, her headgear was hurriedly removed and tied viciously around her stomach, her ear-rings vanished, as did her slippers and her war-chant amidst the uproar was, 'shi, shi le kun' - which means, open, open the door. 'O pa mi leni,' 'you must kill me today.'

By this time, everybody was laughing and shouting with the result that people in the other coaches that managed to squeeze into our coach to find out what was the matter joined in the laugh and relayed commentaries of battle to the various allied camps.

The man later emerged zipping up his fly. The damning evidence! We all had thought the man was joking. Before anyone could say 'garri', the woman had grabbed the man by his shirt and jacked him up a couple of times to the rhythm of 'o pa mi le ni'.

The Ibo man apparently well pleased laughed off his head and interjected quite often, "very good, well done." Some of the passengers later prevailed on the woman to release the man, which she reluctantly did. All this while, the man kept his cool and only warned the woman not to make the mistake of ripping his shirt to shreds. She then immediately dashed into her warehouse cum toilet to re-emerge later confused but calm at which the man now roared off his head like an old Suzuki motorcycle minus the exhaust

He later explained that he had found a fairly manageable toilet in the next compartment and had had the brain wave to teach the miserly Ijebu woman a lesson. So, he shrugged and most of us joined in the laugh because for one, the Ijebu woman was definitely confused for we saw her rearranging her load, not with any desire of releasing the toilet but I guess just to satisfy herself that her eyes have not been befoggled by so many years on a diet of 'garri' and I guess she also needed the time to demobilize and allow her racing heart settle.

Nothing extraordinary happened for some time until we got to Mokwa station. Was Uncle Jack right! It sure was a busy station. Jack could tell you the whole history of the Railway Corporation anytime of the day or night including details of major incidents that made Railway history.

He even knew the day; time and year Lord Lugard first boarded a train from Lagos to Lokoja with his wife.

Among my father's friends, Jack easily stands out. We the children are never bored listening to his many funny tales and anecdotes. He was instrumental to a large extent for my decision to journey by train. He was in the employ of the Railways for twenty years before he finally threw down the coupling-pin for a foreman's helmet with a construction company.

I can still recall his many tales and adventures he had a way of recounting with gusto. A short round-man, round in the sense that his bowlegs coupled with his bouncy gait always gives one the impression that he was a rubber ball on the roll. The hair he lacked on the massive, ever shiny horseshoe shaped baldpate of his, he made up for on his jaw. He had a way of stroking his beard whenever in thought. From the sideburns down to the moustache, coupled with the beard, only one word aptly captured their state - bushy.

Aunty Anuli, anyway, that is how we usually address Jack's wife have tried to get him to shave off the beards several times with no success. I guess the imagined picture of Jack minus his beards would make the Guinness Book of Records. I am sure he would have looked far worse than a cock without its feathers. She only succeeded in extracting from him a promise to have his beard and hair trimmed nicely every 17th of October; it being their wedding anniversary. Incidentally too, Uncle Jack only within earshot of us the children and Jack behind his back hated seeing the few strands that seem to multiply astronomically anytime Aunty Anuli attempted shaving off the offensive beard that annoyingly emphasizes her double chin.

There were many tales of the many attempts Jack made to get rid of his wife's annoying beard. The most funny one being when he sort the advice of my dad and carried out the coup d'essai. She has had to let the beard be to prevent it spreading further. The story goes that Jack had bought a depilatory cream, hid it and for once, devoted the whole day to reminding Aunty Anuli of their courting days. They had visited the amusement park, the museum and even the Bar Beach. In the evening, Aunty Anuli had come over to our house to recount her trilling experience to my mum. My mum must have been envious of such thoughtfulness and care from Jack because I recall her saying to my dad, "Have you heard of how Jack has been taking care of Anuli?"

"And so what? Are they not married?"

"Hen hen! When was the last time you took me out to drink pepper soup and stout? Or are you of the notion that wooing a woman into wedlock means that she deserves less attention. Today, today, you must take me to Pintos for ice cream and 'Jolly Mama' for pepper soup. I hope you have heard me Agada!"

"No problem, so long as you promise to foot the bill or agree that the treat replace the 'Aso Oke' dress you've been on my neck to buy for you."

My dad had sort refuge in the bedroom when Aunty Anuli joined her voice to her friend's in demanding the night out. My old man had emerged about five minutes later with my mum in tow, having succumbed to the combined firepower of the women to the night out. I was happy for mum and happy that I will get to boss my sisters around over dinner too so that I can get my way with the soup pot.

I ate my fill that night but almost got my old man's belt applied to my behind the next day, for eating the gizzard he was reserving for himself.

Anyway, Aunty Anuli informed my mum that Jack would not be coming over to our house that night because he promised taking her out too. Well, the story goes that Aunty Anuli had too much to drink and Jack was the happier for it and to crown it all, Aunty Anuli had woken up the next morning without her beard. She had given Jack hell before finally being convinced and won over with many presents that she looked better without it. Her conviction had been short lived as the beard came out with a determination and spread which led her to let it be according to her, on doctor's advice, but most likely to spite Jack and keep his attention. The story goes that anytime Anuli complains about the bushiness of her husband's beards, Jack's conditionality was always the same, "Only witches grow beards. Shave off yours and I will shave off mine minus the moustache."

"You know that is impossible. Anytime I try shaving, it only gets worse. Kindly stop calling me or inferring that I am a witch on account of my few stands of hair; I don't like it"

Come every October 17"', Jack normally tries staying off from the company, the jolly trio Ombu, Agada and Jack but Aunty Anuli was ever on her guard as they say 'once shaved twice weary'. Most time, Jack and Ombu are usually at our place, most likely in deference to my dad's age. Though he was only two day's senior to Jack and a week to Ombu, he never the less fails to claim his eldership especially when kola and wine needs to be blessed.

Most times, Jack reminiscences about the good old days of the railways in Nigeria and the grand conspiracy that led to the derailment of a dream train from ever reaching its station.

According to Jack, when Nigeria gained independence from the British and the First Republic of politicians were ousted from office via the barrel of the gun of some 'miscreants in army uniform' that ultimately led to The Queen of England inviting General Yakubu to England, not out of love for the uniform but in a bid to protect British interests and investment in Nigeria.

So the Queen summoned, and Yakubu had to be hurriedly groomed before jetting off to see the Queen. They were said to have discussed; but Jack insists that what transpired must have been in the mode of, "If you promise to help safe – guard our interest in Nigeria, then the United Kingdom will do all in its might to help you put down the rebels in the eastern part of Nigeria."

With the promise strengthened into a pact, signed and kept, Yakubu had gone sightseeing and had been so impressed by the British Railway system of transportation that immediately he got back to Nigeria, he had sent an ad – hoc committee back to England to understudy the rail system in Britain with a view of establishing such a system in Nigeria. The committee went to England, saw

17

the wondrous accomplishment of and capabilities of the 'iron-snake' and submitted a comprehensive report to the Green General Yakubu.

He made so much noise about his dream of revolutionizing the rail system in Nigeria that with the civil disturbance in the Eastern part of the Country successfully put out with the surrender of the rebels, the Northern Elders brain-stormed and arrived at the following conclusion:

"If the railway is allowed to be given priority over and above other means of transportation, then the North will be at a disadvantage in the sense that Nigeria's main exports of oil, coal, cocoa, timber, rubber, tin, palm-oil were to be found in the Western, Eastern and Southern parts of the country. This then means that the North will be the worse off on the long run. The railways will help in speeding up development of these areas and since the North could only boast of fast vanishing pyramids of groundnut and other farm produce like hides and skin, the West would wield too strong an economic hold on the country to make nonsense of the Northern hold of political power. More so, the north had no big rivers a ferry could profitably ply as obtains in the South, East and West. Another reason why Yakubu's dream had to be but a dream was the fact that the North was still educationally trying unsuccessfully to bridge the gap between the North and the rest of the country.

So, according to Uncle Jack, Yakubu was finally convinced after lots of meetings to replace his dream of having an efficient rail system with that of an efficient road system. Dual carriage – ways were advocated but when the government pointed out that moving oil – its main export and foreign exchange earner from the Southern/Eastern axis of the country to other parts of the country would cost more if done by road than by rail, the North pointed out that they will provide tankers and thus be able to have a foot hold in the economic strength of Nigeria by thus benefiting from the oil windfall. Thus Northern millionaires will be made, the road network will further open up the North with other parts of the country, and the North will thus have a strong political and economic hold in Nigeria to its advantage which will thus facilitate the eventually catching-up of the North educationally with the rest of the country.

So Yakubu sold out his dream station for a road network. The existing railways thus remained its old self as left by the colonial masters. Locomotives that had transversed the key colonial routes in search of raw materials for companies in the United Kingdom and in moving its troops up and down Nigeria were those still in existence in present day Nigeria. Except for a few coaches ordered from India with no thought given to the procurement of spare parts and the full reactivation of the Railways' Workshop, the Railway remained it old self and like the camel its totem, it patiently bore the rot, the thirst for modernization while plodding on through time with its load of antiquities.

The infrastructural facilities decayed, staff salaries were owed, pensioners retired and resigned to a life of penury, bad debts and death in ignominy. Uncle Jack read the signs on the walls of his many coaches and decided to quit while he was still 'Locus Mentis'. He did and found a new love and boss – building and Mega Star Constructions.

So, Monday came and I decided to go and see Zaria by train while hoping to have an experience that would surpass any of Uncle Jack's.

Do I remember the station! The platform was filled with intending passengers anxious to see Kano by train, not for its comfort but because it happens to be far cheaper than going by road or even by air.

Those with loads struck deals with the station waifs to help them secure a seat with the result that immediately these waifs called 'Almageris' see someone get-up, preparatory to disembarking, they immediately fill the partially vacated seat to the inconvenience of those disembarking and those continuing. When some Kano bound passengers noticed this, they themselves started hoarding the vacated seats for their own convenience by immediately putting a bag or whatnot on the seat as a sign of its occupancy. On this particular train, a bunch of roses would have been less appealing than an offered seat to a lady in distress. Those with loads struggled to get their loads on board first and foremost, then, they go in search of their employed waifs. When they find him, they thank him and tell him to keep the seat warm a while longer so that they could effect the transfer of their loads to the right coach, and thus seat secure to Kano. Those with loads but no seat insurance pursue the stopping train with their loads on heads and in their hands; these generally constitute the aisle locusts. Those with real loads that will take two or more trips to get them on board generally constitute the toilet converters; and women rule this echelon.

Well, the train chugged into Mokwa station exactly at 3:45 pm the next day and we saw so many heads, so many running legs and heard so many mouths running all at once.

With the cries, shouts and wailing of those alighting and those competing for the use of the doors into the train, we that were passing through, especially people like myself taking their first ride on a train starred, gawped and marveled at this experience.

We took in more souls, more loads and a new locomotive to help the tired one that had pulled and chugged thus far from Lagos. My coach saw some new faces. The Ibo man got down at Mokwa as did the action-man, but Mama Ijebu was still very much in possession of the toilet and now a seat. Some beggars joined my coach; at least they dressed and behaved beggarly. A fat mother with a nursing baby also joined my coach and in fact shared the aisle seat on which I was seating with me. She sat facing our destination while I retained my window seat.

It was around midnight when it happened. By then, the train made all the noise and many heads found their chest, some their palms and some, other sleeping shoulders. So also did many weary eyes sort to shut out their immediate presence. Some did, some aspired to by noting and nodding, and some eyes just shone in silence.

I couldn't sleep. I had dozed during the day and my legs – my calves especially were hurting from maintaining their reassuring touch with my two bags directly under the seat. Perhaps it was due to the many tales I have heard about night robberies on trains where robbers take advantage of dulled senses by making off with any bag that catches their interest with the dozer none the wiser until he wakes, reaches his station and remembers his kept burden, or just my curiosity to see all and miss none. I don't know. It could possibly have been a brew of the two that made my eyes keep learning about and around my person.

Anyway, the aisle still was just a name as even the checkers found out when they had made their many climbs through the train. It was then that professed beggars found their voices and kept up a pleading chant of "Ba bi Allah" which guaranteed no molestation and ejection from the checkers.

One particular beggar-when-the-checkers-were-around-only had caught my attention since he boarded the train at Mokwa. He was admittedly dirty, had a bad case of bromopnea, very ragged and was the only beggar I saw with a very big and dirty pillow for a bundle.

In fact, this pillow was so dirty and smelly that it had generated some arguments immediately the train pulled out of the station; for the beggar had no intention of being uncomfortable on his free ride to Kano and so had used his evil smelling dirty pillow and garb to create a squatting space which he expanded to take his person in a prone position. He would deliberately raise his pillow, and those around him in trying to escape the stench found new places for themselves to the beggar's front and back and the beggar would smile, exposing his kola red scattered mandibles. He sure exploited his state. Amidst curses, hisses and angry explosions from both the standing and the seated, the beggar claimed his prize and managed to sleep on the aisle with his head comfortable on his smelly pillow and his legs tugged in a little bit.

One of his greatest antagonists was a fat woman who claimed that the smell was responsible for her baby's continued cry. Even after offering the disturbing mouth a giant size breast, which I couldn't help but stare at, the baby continually announced its discomfort. I found myself thinking how lucky the baby was and imagining what human milk must taste like. The cry had grown strident and the fat woman who must have been from Calabar from her accent had to stand, strap the baby to her back and rock it to sleep by a curious dance.

The beggar did not help issues by trying to cluck the little wailer to submission; for the mother took offence, as did most of us at his smell and frightful mien his face especially, took when he grinned benevolently at the baby. The woman had not spared the beggar by abusing and cursing him first in English which tapered into pidgin and when I guess she found both wanting, she said her piece in vernacular which confirmed my earlier summation of her being a Calabar woman. With the try and failure of the beggar to do good in making the baby stop it's wailing, he shrugged, cursed back in Hausa and made himself comfortable once more. We knew no peace until the baby succumbed to sleep and thus the woman could sit down once more after transferring the little king from her back to her laps and thus her legs took a break but not her mean look which should have turned the beggar to stone.

The baby finally found sleep and soon others followed suit and by midnight nearly all were asleep and only the harsh but lolling sound of wheels on rails woke the night. The beggar got up and moved to the end of the coach most likely due to the need for privacy. He squatted to spray and cool the rails with his piss.

Immediately he left, the woman had got up too, placed her sleeping baby on her seat, took a cup from the bag under her seat ostensively to go and get water. She woke some and managed to get through. Now, the beggar had placed his pillow just a seat in distance from the nearest exit and the woman in passing stumbled and somehow kicked the beggar's pillow into the night.

The beggar's cry from his squatty position woke most if not all in the train. He had pulled up his trousers, tied them and raced to the exit in question. He clutched at the frames wailing, starring into the night. All I could make out of his gibbering were the word 'Walahi' Walahi-talai".

The woman was saying her sorries and pleadings in English and pidgin. She even learnt the Hausa word 'Sanu, hakuri' meaning 'sorry' from the man that threw more light on the situation. He understood Hausa and was able to make-out the beggar's tale in pain while he relayed the woman's plea to him in Hausa.

Our able interpreter was able to inform us that the rather unusual wailing over a lost pillow that the woman had offered to replace by paying the beggar an amount that should get the beggar a new pillow was due to the fact that the pillow was no pillow but a bank. According to the man, all the money the beggar whom we now learnt was a herdsman had made from the sale of his cows he claimed to have been lodged within the vaults of stench. The beggar herdsman was claiming to have lost over three hundred thousand naira. The immediate reaction of most was that the train be stopped, but before then, this slow train suddenly seemed to have been done a world of good by the new locomotive which must have been pulling the sixteen coaches at a speed of 80 – 90 kilometers an hour by my estimation; for now bushes, lights and towns were whirling past and no longer waving bye. The tale, the noise, its deciphering and its dissemination must have taken another five minutes and prospects of trekking back miles into nothingness, trying to disrobe the night in a bid to find the pillow-bank was disheartening and moreover, it would have to be morning before the search could take off properly assuming the train thus agrees to stop but no one, especially those that were bound for Kano who have been sitting for over a day now relished the prospect of continuing their sitting into two/three days.

And worse of all, the passengers were not totally bought over by this tale. Some claimed the pillow couldn't have had nothing but cow-piss in it, others that it couldn't have been holding more than a hundred thousand naira and one man in particular that I remember to have been rather silent all the way from Lagos suddenly turned very vocal. Shouting and preaching a doctrine that must have been christened. 'The Law of Karma". He told us that it was bound to happen due to the miserly act of the beggar.

"Why," he asked, "should a man with so much try dodging paying his fares which cost less than a hundred naira for his ticket to Kano!"

The Karma priest, who I must confess, was rather muscular barred any from pulling the chain claimed at guaranteeing the deceleration of the train and its eventual stopping.

The beggar wailed, the trained buzzed and kept chasing the night. The fat woman, from her pleas now adopted a new chant, "Na lie", for the prospect of paying such an amount was rather converting. Yes, converting because even a devout Christian would and couldn't have helped shouting 'Na lie' too even if the pillow had contained that much.

She took her seat with some saying, "'No mind am, na thief'." How he go come begin lie say that pillow wey he pick for gutter contain over three hundred thousand.' Who dash am the money? Where he get am?'"

And some believed that the pillow could have had that much, and the man could have had that much with him for according to them,

"Make una no talk so, una know how much them dey sell ordinary one cow now?"

A voice authoritatively claimed that a cow, no matter how small these days, sold for nothing less than ten thousand naira and as high as twenty thousand naira. So the debate was on, the train was on the run, the tears were rolling, Fingers were snapping in anguish, commentaries and arguments spread from coach four through the train and even the checkers came back to see the rich beggar.

All this while, the conversation was mostly in Pidgin English. This was the common front on which all diverse tongues felt a little bit at home and at ease in understanding one another. This was the universal tongue of the poor and semi-literate who outnumber the educated elites that speak the Queen's English fluently but with noticeable colorations of the mother tongue. Thus when a Northerner speaks, the pronunciation or words are heard distinctly colored by his mother tongue. I recall that my former teacher a Hausa explained his inability to pronounce the word 'people' correctly due to the fact that his mother tongue's alphabet has an 'f' for a 'p' and thus "people" always come out as "feofle" amidst stifled laughs. Mr. Gyang, the History teacher was from the Middle Belt and pronounced 'Reggae Music' as "Leggae Music". A typical 'Esan' person from the Mid-West will pronounce the name "John" as "Gyon" for the same obvious reasons and Nigeria happens to house over a thousand dialects.

With time, the arguments ceased, the Karma priest lost ears and finally sat down. Curious legs, eyes and voices returned to their coaches. The fat woman momentarily forgot her fear voiced in her "Ehs!" and "Ahs!" and the disturbing "Three hundred thousand naira!" by her fitful dozing. Judges retired into their slumber, but the cow merchant now cried inside. A cry that sees no tears but only a binding festering sore of the soul.

The train forgot that the beggar was wounded. The sore was allowed to fester and gangrene set in. He bore the pain in his impotence, sat clutching his knees while he seethed. His eyeballs became gleaming red-hot coals. He rocked slowly, to and fro, and yet he hardly moved. You would have had to look hard at the beggar to discern the slight sway to and fro to the rhythm of a soul in deep distress. He couldn't have been comfortable yet he sat totally indifferent to personal discomfort. He managed to keep out of people's way or rather; the people sensing what he must be going through let him be. So he sat, he seethed; he waited and grabbed the opportunity of avenging his lost vault when it presented itself. All must have slept or dozed or like myself, been in the state of "wassle" - midway between sleep and wakefulness, usually caused by fatigue and lack of sleep.

The coach was peopled mainly by southerners, Easterners, and Westerners and the Northern voices that had heard and come to sympathize with the beggar, had spoken angrily in Hausa and left.

The woman was advised to get down at any station the train pulls into by dawn while the beggar would be kept on board, one way or another until he reaches his unpaid for destination Kano. But the beggar knew sleep no more. He sat with his hands hugging his knees, his eyes mirrored his teeth, and his head shook at intervals. He sat wailing, silent but seething. Around three (3:00am.) he struck! Even I must have dozed.

All I saw when I was brought back to full consciousness by the baby's cry and then the woman's was the beggar with a bundle at the door. Next, the bundle sailed into the night leaving in its wake the startled cry of one rudely and frighteningly woken from the sleep of the innocent. It was a small voice crying out in anguish yet it was surprisingly loud. Loud enough to have woken most bowed heads in coach four anyway.

The beggar was rooted to the exit. He stood holding the doorframe fulfilled. He turned from grinning into the night to face his captivated audience and like a pleased saint, said in a surprisingly loud, booming and dreadful voice,

"Ka chuce ni, I'li ma na ye nawa, Allah baza! Damuba."

Then the train went mad!

www.ingramcontent.com/pod-product-compliance
Lightning Source LLC
Chambersburg PA
CBHW051928220626
47052CB00003B/630